THE CREEPER DIARIES

BOOK EIGHT

MOB SCHOOL SWAP

Also by Greyson Mann

THE CREEPER DIARIES

BOOK EIGHT

MOB SCHOOL SWAP

GREYSON MANN
ILLUSTRATED BY AMANDA BRACK

Sky Pony Press
New York

THE CREEPER DIARIES: MOB SCHOOL SWAP. Copyright © 2019 by Hollan Publishing, Inc.

Minecraft® is a registered trademark of Notch Development AB. The Minecraft game is copyright © Mojang AB.

Sky Pony Press books may be purchased in bulk at special discounts for sales promotion, corporate gifts, fund-raising, or educational purposes. Special editions can also be created to specifications. For details, contact the Special Sales Department, Sky Pony Press, 307 West 36th Street, 11th Floor, New York, NY 10018 or info@skyhorsepublishing.com.

Sky Pony® is a registered trademark of Skyhorse Publishing, Inc.®, a Delaware corporation.

Visit our website at www.skyponypress.com.

10 9 8 7 6 5 4 3 2 1

Library of Congress Cataloging-in-Publication Data is available on file.

Special thanks to Erin L. Falligant.

Cover illustration by Amanda Brack
Cover design by Brian Peterson

Hardcover ISBN: 978-1-5107-3751-8
E-book ISBN: 978-1-5107-3755-6

Printed in the United States of America

DAY 1: TUESDAY

I *have always, always, ALWAYS wanted a brother.*

When my baby sister Cammy was born, I went on strike. I locked myself in my room and wouldn't come out for a WHOLE night. Not even for Mom's burnt pork chops and roasted potatoes. No sirree.

I mean, COME ON. I already had two sisters. What were the chances that creeper egg would crack open and deliver ANOTHER girl creeper? But it did.

And I'm not gonna lie—I might have shed a tear or two, mourning the long-lost brother that I, Gerald Creeper Jr., was never going to have.

But that all changed last week. See, Mom decided we should take part in a Mob School Swap. That's when a mob from another school in the Overworld comes to live with our family for like a month. "He can share a room with you, Gerald," said Mom. "Like brothers!"

Well, I nearly busted out my dance moves when I heard that. Yup, I was celebrating alright. It was almost January—the start of a new year at Mob

Middle School. And I'd be going back to school with a BROTHER.

I told my best friend, Sam Slime, about it right away. I mean, good news like that could destroy a guy if he tried to keep it all inside.

Then I cleaned my room from top to bottom. I moved my squid Sticky's aquarium to one end of the dresser and told Sticky that soon—VERY soon—we'd have a brother. Maybe even another creeper like me, or like my old buddy Cash who moved away a year ago.

But guess who showed up bright and early on our doorstep this morning? A creeper like Cash?

Nope.

A slime like Sam?

Nope.

An Enderman like Eddy, the coolest kid at school?

Ah, no. Not even close.

A zombie? A witch? A skeleton? A spider jockey?

Nuh-uh. You can keep guessing all night long, and you'll NEVER get it right.

Mom said it would be a surprise. Well, I was surprised all right when I opened the front door and saw a HUMAN standing there.

Yup, you heard me. A HUMAN!!! This scrawny brown-haired kid in a cape stood on our front step, looking like a squished bug under his heavy backpack.

Now let's get one thing straight: creepers and humans do NOT hang out. EVER. I mean, except for when my big sister Cate was crushing on some human named Steve. She even started DRESSING like a human for a while, but we don't talk about that. At least not in front of Dad.

Anyway, turns out this kid's name is Andrew and he's from Humanville. You know where that is? I sure do. My family got lost in Humanville last summer, when Dad took a wrong turn with the minecart. And let me tell you, those humans were not the least bit friendly to a bunch of creepers like us.

So why'd Mom go and invite a human to come LIVE here? And while we're asking the tough questions, why would Andrew WANT to come live with a bunch of creepers, anyway?

I would have asked, except Andrew started sneezing,
right there in the doorway. He sprayed me good
before Mom finally pulled him inside to get warm.

But getting warm sure didn't cure Andrew's sneezing.
Turns out, he has allergies. He sneezed, wheezed,

and sniffled all the way through breakfast. He's a
very drippy dude. GREAT. I'll be bringing a giant red
nose to school with me tomorrow. Maybe he'll be so
gross and drippy that he'll pass for a zombie.

And surprise, surprise—I learned right away that
Andrew and I have NOTHING in common. I have three
sisters, but Andrew is an only child (some mobs get all

the luck). I love rap music, but Andrew isn't all that into music. NOPE. He loves some weird extracurricular called "hockey." He even showed me the hockey stick that had been poking out of his backpack. It's bent at the end, like a broken wooden sword.

But here's the real kicker: I love burnt pork chops. Love, love, LOVE them. But Andrew? He does NOT like his pork chops burned to a crisp. In fact, he doesn't like pork chops at all—or any kind of meat for that matter. He's a VEGETARIAN.

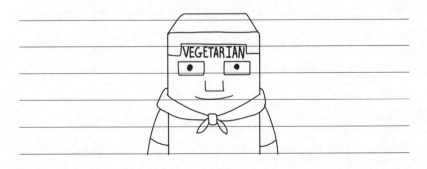

I guess his parents grow organic vegetables on a farm outside of Humanville. As soon as the V-word popped out of Andrew's mouth, I wanted to stuff it back in. We do NOT mention vegetables at the dinner table—not after Mom's "go green" kick a while back. She served nothing but Brussels sprouts for like a month!

So while Mom warmed up some mushroom stew for Andrew, I made a big show of telling her how especially TASTY her burnt pork chops were this morning. I'm pretty sure Andrew wrinkled up his nose when I mentioned the chops, or maybe he was just holding back a sneeze.

Mom was sure bending over backward to make Andrew feel at home here. And Dad told even more

corny jokes than usual, even though they were
bombing left and right.

"Mrs. Creeper always says, when life hands you
moldy mushrooms, make mushroom stew!" said Dad,
all cheerful-like.

"MOLDY mushrooms?" said Andrew. There was that
nose wrinkle again.

"I'll bet you're tired after your trip, son. Creepers need
their sleepers. And humans need to shut their peepers!"

"Sleep? In the middle of the day?" asked Andrew,
his "peepers" wide open.

My sisters were trying WAY too hard with Andrew, too. Cate asked all kinds of questions about his family. Maybe she hoped he had an older brother named Steve. And Cammy studied Andrew like a shiny new toy. She was so into Andrew that we actually made it through a whole meal without the Exploding Baby throwing a temper tantrum.

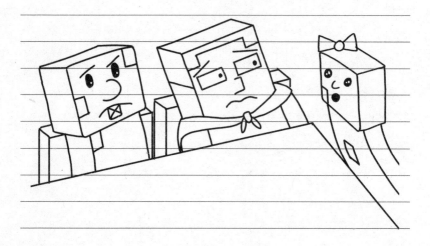

The only sister who acted NORMAL around Andrew was my Evil Twin, Chloe. I could hear her hissing from all the way across the table. Mom hissed something right back at her about keeping an open mind and making friends with mobs who aren't "just like us."

But Chloe wasn't having it. And for once, I actually agreed with her. I mean, what was Mom THINKING, inviting Andrew here? How was I supposed to bring this kid to school with me???

I could see it already—heading back to Mob Middle School with this dude in a cape glued to my side. Every mob would be staring and whispering. Bones and his gang of spider jockeys would be pointing and poking at us with their bony fingers. And I already had enough trouble keeping those bony jocks off my back.

Things only got worse at bedtime. Andrew leaned his hockey stick against the wall and then pulled this thing out of his trunk that nearly blinded me. I guess it was his lucky rock. Glowstone, he called it— something his dad brought back from a mining trip in the Nether. And Andrew set it RIGHT on the dresser next to Sticky.

Was he just going to LEAVE it there? All day long? The thing glowed like a beacon even in the daytime. How was a creeper supposed to get his sleepers???

Now I like to think I'm an understanding creeper. I keep my lucky petrified mushroom pretty close to me at all times, too. But my mushroom never blinded a guy when he was trying to get some shut-eye. SHEESH.

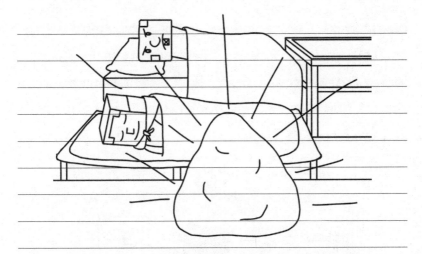

And did I mention that Andrew's trunk takes up half the room? I thought he was going to empty it out and then let Dad take it out to the garage. But he didn't. He took out his glowstone, and then he locked that trunk back up—as if it were full of stolen treasure or something.

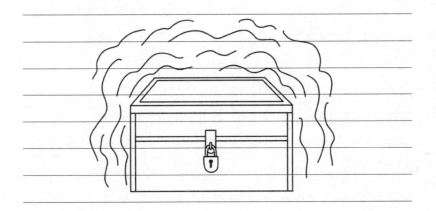

Did he think I was going to SNOOP in there? Well, I wasn't. At least not until I heard the click of the lock. After that, the ONLY thing I wanted to do was snoop. That's the thing about locks. They just make you want to bust them open.

"Whatcha got in that trunk?" I asked, sounding all cool and casual like.

He blew his nose and shrugged. "Some stuff my parents sent with me. It's no big deal."

But I could tell by the tone of his voice that it WAS a big deal. I'm a pretty good detective—like Sherlock Bones in those mystery books. Whenever my buddy Sam is even THINKING about telling a lie, I can spot it coming from a mile away.

Lie Detector

So now I'm trying to sleep, but Andrew is sniffling and snorting in the bed beside me. His precious glowstone is burning right through my eyelids. I can't stop wondering what's locked up in that chest. And every time I even THINK about taking Andrew to school with me tomorrow, I start to sweat.

It feels like I'm starting Mob Middle School all over again. (And let me tell you, that is NOT a part of my life I want to do over.) When I was a scrawny sixth grader, I didn't think I'd survive my first month. Bones and his buddies slapped a nickname on me: they started calling me Itchy (because I have this little problem with itchy skin), and that name stuck like mold on a mushroom. So Bones and his buddies are going to eat Andrew alive for sure—and then have ME for dessert.

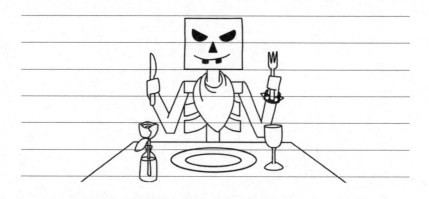

This creeper needs a plan—a way to survive thirty days with a human "brother." Luckily, I keep my trusty journal under my mattress for times like this. So now I'm staring into that glowstone, just waiting for a few genius ideas to strike.

I gotta find a way to make Andrew seem more NORMAL. You know, maybe help him ditch the cape. And stop all that sniffling.

Maybe I can even help him look tough, like a spider jockey. He may not ride spiders or swing swords, but he says he's pretty good with a hockey stick. (Note to self: figure out what this hockey thing is all about. Is that hockey stick a weapon?)

Maybe I'll get lucky and Andrew WILL have loads of gemstones in that chest! Because if he does, Bones will be falling all over himself trying to buddy up to Andrew. EVERY mob will. And as his brother and agent, I could cash in on that popularity. Just sayin' . . .

Okay, I think I've got a plan. Here goes:

> # 30-Day Plan for Surviving the Swap
>
> - Give Andrew a makeover. (Ask Cate for help.)
> - Figure out what he's allergic to. STOP the drip!
> - Learn more about this hockey thing.
> - Get inside that locked trunk. Is Andrew rich???

I sure hope this plan works. Because if it doesn't—if Andrew tanks at Mob Middle School and takes me down with him—I might have to pack it up and move to Humanville.

DAY 2: WEDNESDAY

Okay, I'm glad I have at least ONE sister. One sister with a very big closet.

After we woke up last night, I dragged Andrew straight into Cate's room. Her closet is like a whole other Overworld—with racks of skins that could transform a creeper into anything he wanted to be. And hopefully transform a human, too.

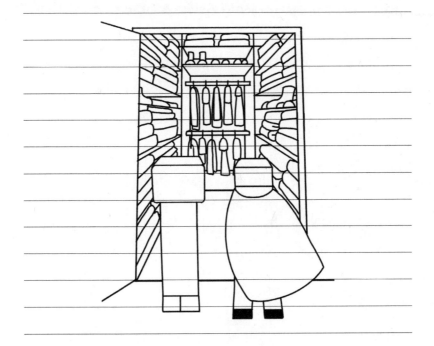

At first, Cate's ideas were way over the top. She wanted to dress up Andrew like a zombie pigman, until I told her that going to school with a zombie pigman was ALMOST as bad as going to school with a human. I said that last part kind of loud, which I was sorry about, because Andrew heard me. But maybe it's best that he know the truth. This is NOT going to be an easy road for the kid. Luckily, he has Gerald Creeper Jr. by his side.

So we settled on dressing Andrew all in green. That way, if he's walking down the hall between me and Sam Slime, maybe he'll blend right in and no one will even notice him. A creeper can hope, right?

Mom did a double-take when Andrew showed up at the dinner table dressed like a creeper. But then Cate danced into the room wearing her red wig— her HUMAN wig. And Dad started hissing, and then everyone forgot all about Andrew's clothes.

I used to call Cate's wig "Rosy" because it's just SO red. And while I ate my chops at dinner, I started thinking about names. And nicknames. And how to make sure Andrew didn't get slapped with a nickname like "Itchy" during his first few days at Mob Middle School.

See, I was named after my dad, Gerald Creeper
Sr. And after Grandpa Gerald. And Great-Grandpa
Gerald. And Great-Great Grandpa Gerald, who's kind
of famous around these parts for starting the first
Overworld Games.

None of my relatives went by "Gerry" or "Ger"
or "G." Not a single one of them. So I went by
"Gerald" too. I mean, I didn't really have a choice.

But maybe Andrew did. I studied the kid and tried on
a few nicknames, just for size.

He wasn't going to make this easy for me, I could tell.
So I settled on calling him "dude" every chance I got.

Like tonight, when it was time to get up for school,
I nudged his shoulder.

And he was all like, "Huh?" He rubbed his eyes, looked out the window, and said, "But it's dark out!" I guess this whole sleep-in-the-day-and-go-to-school-at-night deal isn't how things work in Humanville.

Andrew was so sleepy that he must have forgotten all about the green clothes Cate and I had found for him. He put his blue T-shirt and jeans back on instead. When he reached for his cape, I had to step in and take control. "No cape, my dude. Remember the clothes we picked out for you?"

But he said he couldn't wear those because they were CRUSTY. Say WHAT???

Andrew showed me how he'd sneezed all over Cate's green T-shirt. Sure enough, the thing looked like Ziggy Zombie's napkin after lunch. GROSS.

So much for dressing the dude like a creeper.

Anyway, now it's time to leave for school, and I've gotta say, I've got a bad feeling in my gut about this.

Wish me luck.

DAY 3: THURSDAY

Well, at least we got THAT over with—my first day of bringing a human with me to Mob Middle School. It felt a lot like the day I brought my squid Sticky to school, only to find out that it was NOT Take Your Squid to School Day. But that's a whole other story.

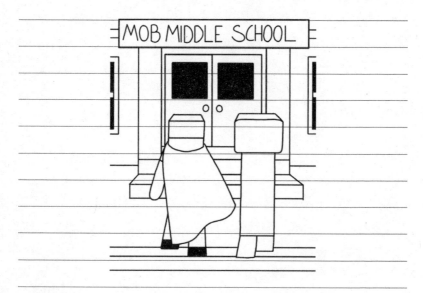

Things started out EXACTLY the way I thought they would. Every single mob in that hallway spun around and stared when Andrew and I walked through the door. I could see the news lighting up the hall like a Redstone circuit.

And then suddenly Emma Enderman was beside us, asking if she could write an article about Andrew for the school newspaper. That girl's got a future in reporting, for sure. She got right up in Andrew's face before anyone else could get to him.

I tried to take charge of the interview. I mean, I used to write for the MOB MIDDLE SCHOOL OBSERVER too, so I'm a whiz at steering stories in the right direction. "Ask him about hockey," I told Emma.

But she totally ignored me. She kept asking Andrew about his family and about Humanville—you know, the facts I DIDN'T want to focus on. "The dude doesn't want to talk about that stuff," I told Emma. "Oh, and did I mention he goes by 'Dude'?"

When she took Andrew's picture, I photo-bombed the shot and scrunched down low, trying to make Andrew look taller and tougher. He gave me a weird look, but I didn't care. A brother's gotta do what a brother's gotta do, right?

When Sam spotted us, he bounced over—and then wiggled to a stop in front of Andrew. I swear, I've never seen that slime look more surprised.

Sam was all like, "Oh! You're a . . . I mean . . . Gerald, why didn't you tell me that . . . I mean, um . . . nice to meet you."

I let the slime sweat it out for a while before saving him. "Sam, meet my dude Andrew." Then I pushed them both along the hall toward first period, hoping to avoid any skeletons and spider jockeys along the way.

We kept a low profile till lunchtime. But it's kind of hard to hide a human in the cafeteria. A spotlight was shining down on Andrew, I swear. Every witch, zombie, and skeleton in the room caught every embarrassing thing he did. Even TEACHERS stopped to stare.

When Andrew sneezed and blew his lunch bag right off the table, mobs watched. When he wiped his nose on his cape, mobs stared. And when he fell asleep in his mushroom stew, mobs snickered.

Sam, of all mobs, should have known about THOSE. He's pretty much allergic to milk. "Lactose intolerant," he calls it, which means the slime has to steer clear of milk and cheese or he gets really gassy. And really stinky. FAST.

"What's he allergic to?" asked Sam. "Mushrooms?"

"Mushrooms?" I hissed. "Seriously, Sam?" I mean, who's allergic to mushrooms? But then I saw Andrew's face nodding off in that stew again, and I started to wonder. I mean, it's pretty much ALL Mom's been feeding him since he got to our house. And he just gets stuffier and sneezier. So . . . who knows?

Anyway, when Ziggy Zombie sat down next to us,
Andrew woke right up—and screamed like a ghast in the
Nether. Did I mention that he's TERRIFIED of zombies?
It's the weirdest thing. I mean, Ziggy is as harmless as
a silverfish. He's gross, for sure—and totally annoying.
But scary? No way. I just don't get it.

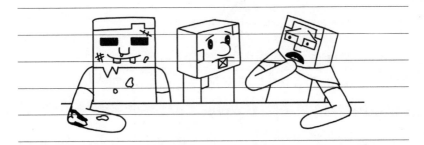

But every time Ziggy made a move, Andrew flinched.
And Ziggy thought that was HILARIOUS. He moaned
and groaned, trying to spook Andrew even more. I
gotta say, I saw a whole other side to that zombie
last night. And it wasn't pretty.

But enough about Ziggy. He was the least of our
problems. Because as soon as Bones and his buddies
rattled into the cafeteria, Bones zeroed in on
Andrew. He was beside us in a flash—faster than a
teleporting Enderman.

I kicked Andrew's chair, trying to warn him to sit up straight, or stop sniffling, or SOMETHING. But you know what that boy did? He looked up at Bones, smiled wide, and . . . sneezed.

I'm pretty sure he sprayed Bones right in the eye socket, because next thing I knew, Bones was grunting and growling.

"This is Andrew," Sam said super-fast, as if that slime stood a chance at defending ANY mob against Bones.

"AN-drew?" spat Bones, wiping his face again. "More like DRIPPY Drew. Nice friend you got there,

Itchy." And with that, he walked away, his bones clattering and clanking with each irritated step.

So somehow, in three seconds flat, Bones gave me and Drippy Drew our first and ONLY thing in common: bad nicknames.

SUPER.

At least we got through day one. Only a month left, right? Mom is always telling me to look on the bright side (which is pretty much all I CAN do now that a glowstone lights up my bedroom like a ginormous torch).

So I tried to put on a happy face at breakfast. Until Mom served up more mushroom stew. AGAIN???

I mentioned to Mom that maybe Andrew was allergic to stew and that she should try something NEW. (You know, like MEAT.) But Andrew pretty much dove into that stew, and when he came up for air, he said that he was definitely not allergic to mushrooms. "We grow them at home," he said, all sniffly like.

Then Dad started telling the story of how mobs and humans came together over mushroom stew a gazillion years ago. He usually saves that story for Thanksgiving, but I guess Andrew and the mushroom stew inspired him. So I recited the story along WITH Dad. Why not? I've got every word of it memorized.

". . . In the olden days, only mobs roamed the Overworld, then miners came, and battles broke out. But today, we eat mushroom stew to celebrate the time when mobs and miners finally came together in peace."

Andrew looked up from his stew and wiped his nose. "Huh?"

Turns out, Andrew had learned a DIFFERENT story about the olden days, when only HUMANS

roamed the Overworld. I guess that's what
they teach the kids at school in Humanville anyway.

In the olden days, only humans roamed the Overworld.

When Dad's pie hole dropped open, I fought
the urge to fling a roasted potato into it. He
looked like he was going to argue, but he didn't.
"That's a very interesting story, Andrew," was all
he said.

I'd never seen anyone or anything stop Dad once
he got going on the Story Train. But somehow,
Andrew did.

I couldn't decide if that made him an enemy to my family, or my new hero. Then he coughed up a phlegm ball, and that settled that. Definitely not my hero.

Anyway, Mom took that opportunity to change the subject. "Speaking of coming together," she said, "I was thinking we should invite some friends over for dinner this weekend. Some NEW friends. You know," she said, nudging Dad, "expand our social circles."

NEW friends? Well, that set off nervous fireworks in my chest. Was Mom on some kick now? First, she invited a human to live with us. Was she going to invite EVERY family in Humanville to come dine at our table?

"Ooh," hissed Chloe, "let's invite Cora's family!" Cora is Chloe's best friend. I could take or leave that creeper, but I guess I'd rather eat chops with a family of creepers than a town full of humans.

But Mom shot Chloe down. "I said NEW friends," she repeated. "Different kinds of mobs."

"Like slimes?" I suggested. "We haven't had Sam
and his family over in a while." I crossed my toes,
hoping that suggestion would fly.

But it didn't. Mom was really on a mission here to
"expand our social circles."

Then Cate, in her red wig, piped up and said, "How
about zombie pigmen?"

I think she was joking, but Dad started hissing. Did I
mention Cate went out with a zombie pigman once?

Anyway, Mom lit right up and said, "Yes! How about zombies? That Ziggy Zombie has you over for sleepovers, Gerald. Should we have his family over here?"

"NO!" I hissed. I'd eaten dinner with Ziggy's family, and it's enough to kill a creep's appetite, let me tell you. Rotten flesh everywhere. Moaning and groaning. BLECH.

But somehow, it was already settled. Mom had inked up the calendar and was back at the table in a flash. So now we had something extra special to look forward to on Saturday night. Woo-hoo.

The only thing that made me feel better was spotting snowflakes falling outside the window.

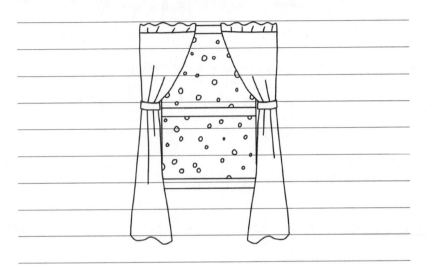

Because snow means sledding.

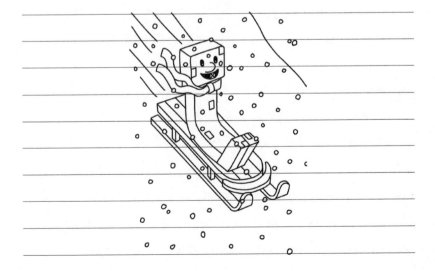

And snow golems.

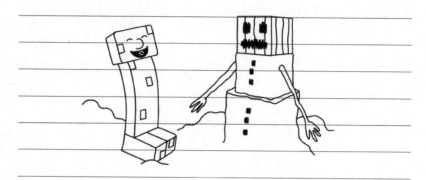

And snowball fights. YAAASSSS!!!

For Dad, it means something TOTALLY different.
"Looks like we'll be shoveling the creeper
cul-de-sac tomorrow, Gerald," he said cheerfully.

I was about to protest when Andrew cleared his
throat. "I'll help you, sir," he said. "I shovel our
hockey rink all the time at home."

HUH?

Now don't get me wrong. I'd do just about anything
to creep out of shovel duty. But watching Andrew
step into my shoes and take over that job felt,
I don't know . . . weird. Especially when Dad said,
"Great, son! And maybe when we're done with the
driveway, we can build you one of those hockey
rinks in the backyard!"

Suddenly, the two of them were in the living room,
sketching out a rink and figuring out where to put
it so that it wouldn't disturb Sock the Sheep. (Did
I mention we have a sheep living in our backyard?
Don't ask.)

45

Anyway, this creeper was suddenly feeling like the odd mob out. I even hissed a little, which I tried to pass off as a burp or a cough.

And that's how I ended up volunteering to HELP Dad and Andrew build that hockey rink. And I don't even know what a hockey rink is.

SHEESH. This is going to be one LONG month.

DAY 4: FRIDAY

Did I mention that Andrew and my squid Sticky are already besties?

Yup. I walk into the room, and Sticky barely looks my way. But when Andrew walks in? Well, you'd think he was Santa Squid himself. Sticky's eyes get bigger than ever, and he floats to the edge of his tank, and he gazes lovingly at Andrew. And Andrew adores Sticky right back. (Sometimes I have to tug on Andrew's cape, just to break up the love fest.)

So I've learned something about Andrew. He loves animals, including Sock the Sheep and even

Sir-Coughs-a-Lot, the hissy cat that lives next door. That got me to thinking: maybe Andrew is allergic to CRITTERS.

See, my buddy Sam found out one day that he's allergic to cats, which is a REAL problem when you love cats as much as Sam does. But then the doctor gave him some medicine, and now he can love up on his cat Moo as much as he wants (which is a LOT, by the way).

So if Andrew is allergic to critters, maybe we can get him some of those miracle meds that stop the drip. See where I'm going with this?

But I had to test out my theory. I didn't really want to hang out in the garage with Sock (which is where Mom puts our sheep when it gets too cold outside). Lucky for me, we have plenty of Sock's wool INSIDE. Mom used to love to knit, and now that it's cold out again, all the sweaters and blankets she knit last year are popping up left and right.

So I asked Mom if she had a wool sweater for Andrew to wear when we went out shoveling snow after school this morning. And of course, she was happy to hurry down the hall to find one. But boy, did that backfire.

Mom came back with the Mooshroom sweater she'd knitted for me. Yup, I actually own a sweater with mushrooms all over it—thanks to Mom.

I thought I'd given that sweater a decent burial in the back of the closet, but Mom found it and helped Andrew wriggle into it. And here's the weird part. Andrew was THRILLED. I guess he's always wanted to see a Mooshroom. So I rest my case—the kid loves critters, and maybe THAT's why his eyes and nose are always oozing.

Anyway, Mom tossed me an old sweater too, which immediately made me itch. But I wasn't worried about my own itchy skin right now. I had my eyes plastered on Andrew, waiting for him to start sneezing or coughing or wheezing, now that he was wrapped in sheep's wool.

But he didn't. I watched and waited for half an hour, while we shoveled. The whole time, he rambled on about hockey rinks and hockey sticks and hockey pucks. And he didn't sneeze at all. Not even ONCE. That's gotta be a new record for him.

So . . . there goes another theory, shot down like a blaze in the Nether. Andrew is NOT allergic to critters—at least not to sheep.

And I did NOT stop the drip. (SNIFF, SNIFFLE, SNEEZE)

DAY 5: SATURDAY MORNING

I was *hoping* Ziggy and *his* family would already have plans this weekend—maybe to stagger over to the nearest town to spook villagers or something. But they didn't. They're definitely coming to dinner tonight. SIGH.

I'm not loving the plan, but Andrew is FREAKING RIGHT OUT. I guess eating lunch with a zombie at school is about all he can handle. Dinner with a whole FAMILY of zombies might put that poor kid right over the edge.

Turns out, Andrew heard about some humans who were attacked by zombies and turned into ZOMBIE VILLAGERS. Well, that sounds like a made-up story—the kind my Evil Twin would spread just to freak out mobs at school. I've tried to tell Andrew all week that Ziggy is harmless.

But Ziggy sure isn't helping things, with his moaning and groaning. I guess the zombie enjoys not being the lowest man on the totem pole anymore. Instead of playing nice, Ziggy has been sneaking up behind Andrew every chance he gets. And Andrew squeals and jumps sky high. Every. Single. Time.

He actually unlocked his trunk this morning for the first time in days. I held my breath and crept over beside him, trying to peek inside. But Andrew was WAY too fast for me. He pulled something out of the trunk and then dropped the lid back down.

Man, that kid is really holding out on me!!! What's he got in there? Secret weapons? A diamond sword? A coat of armor?

He did pull out something shiny, but it wasn't a diamond sword. It was an iron golem, like the kind that tower over villages to protect them from nasty mobs. Except this was a MINI golem. And I guess Andrew got it out of the trunk to protect himself from—you guessed it—ZOMBIES.

That's when I knew he was REALLY scared.

But let's face it, every mob is scared of something. I mean, I'm no fan of spiders. Or cats—especially ocelots, wild cats that lurk in the jungle just waiting to gobble up creepers like me for dinner.

But Andrew isn't scared of ANY of those things. He loves critters! He thought I was LUCKY for running into an ocelot in the jungle last summer. (That's a whole other story. Don't even ask.) Instead, Andrew is scared of the goofiest, grossest mob at school—zombies. Go figure. I don't think I'll ever understand humans.

But here's one thing I know: that iron golem probably won't do much to protect Andrew tonight. So if Ziggy gets out of line, I'm going to have to be the one to step in and do the job.

DAY 5: SATURDAY NIGHT

Mom wanted dinner with the zombies to go perfectly. I tried to tell her that she wasn't being REALISTIC. (It's one of her favorite words. I figured she'd appreciate me using it.) I said there wasn't a single perfect thing about zombies. So why would a dinner with a table FULL of zombies go perfectly?

That's when Mom told me to go clean my room.

Meanwhile, she cleaned the whole house from top to bottom. She arranged the living room just so, with every cushion and cactus in its place.

Personally, I don't think cactus plants have ANY place in a creeper's house, but Mom got on this plant kick last fall. So now, a creeper can barely turn around without getting a pricker in his rear.

She even moved a cactus plant into my BEDROOM, next to Andrew's glowstone. Poor Sticky the Squid is getting squeezed right out—I can barely see the little dude in his aquarium behind all that other stuff.

Anyway, after cleaning the house, Mom made burnt pork chops and roasted potatoes. AND mushroom stew and apple crisp. AND a bowl of carrots—for Andrew, the vegetarian.

I wondered how Mom's menu would go down with Ziggy and his family. I mean Ziggy is all about rotten-flesh sandwiches and rotten-flesh dogs and rotten-flesh fajitas. What was Ziggy going to do with a CARROT?

I found out soon enough. The doorbell rang, and the Zombie Parade began.

Zoe trotted in first. She's a baby zombie and super-fast. Plus, she kind of loves me—the way Sticky loves Andrew.

See, Zoe and I have had some good times. We've
played hide and seek, and rode chickens together—
well, she rode a chicken and I rode a pig, but that's
a whole other story. (We MIGHT have even had tea
parties and rapped nursery rhymes together, but if
you hiss a word of that to ANYONE, I will deny it.)

Old McGerald had a farm, EE-I, EE-I, YO,
And on that farm he had a chicken, EE-I, EE-I, YO.
With a BAWK, BAWK here
And a BAWK, BAWK there,
Here a BAWK, there a BAWK,
Everywhere a BAWK BAWK...

Baby zombies are pretty cute, if you ask me. Too bad they have to grow up and turn into blister-picking, flesh-chomping zombies like Ziggy.

Anyway, Ziggy barely said hello to me. He staggered right past and searched the house for Andrew, who was taking an AWFULLY long time to get dressed in the bedroom. When he finally opened the door, Ziggy was standing RIGHT there, moaning and groaning. Which sent Andrew back inside the bedroom. SLAM!

I would have given Ziggy a talking to, except I was having a freak-out fest of my own. Why? Because

Ziggy and his family hadn't arrived alone. They'd brought their family pet.

A SPIDER.

Yup, Leggy strode in right with Mr. and Mrs. Zombie, as if he'd been on the VIP list or something. As if he owned the place.

Did I mention I'm not a big fan of spiders?

Leggy and I kind of have an understanding when I'm at Ziggy's house. I stay out of his way and he stays out of my way—mostly. But having that spider scuttle across MY living room floor was a whole different thing.

Even Mom eyed that hairy-legged critter with wide eyes. But Mom's the perfect host, right? So she just called everyone to the table and said dinner was ready.

By the time I convinced Andrew to come eat, we had one full table, let me tell you. Six creepers, four zombies, and a human. Oh, and a miniature iron golem.

It was like the first Thanksgiving feast that Dad is always talking about, when mobs and miners came together in peace. Except it WASN'T very peaceful.

First, Mr. Zombie got all excited about the burnt pork chops. "Chops? What a nice surprise!" he said, loading up his plate. "Gerald told us that creepers didn't eat meat on the weekends!"

HUH?

Then it all came back to me—a little white lie I'd told the last time I had dinner at Ziggy's house. See, I was trying to get out of eating rotten flesh, so I'd pretended to be a weekend vegetarian. And it worked! I mean, till now. Lies have a way of sneaking up on a creeper and taking him down.

I started to sweat, which always happens when I get busted. And when I start to sweat, I start to itch.

When Mom saw me scratching my back against the chair (a sure sign of guilt), she shot a few arrows at me with her eyes.

Then she said something to Mr. and Mrs. Zombie about serving meat because tonight was a "special occasion." And she got a few more chops out of the oven.

Leggy must have smelled the chops, because he crept into the room. And I suddenly lost my appetite.

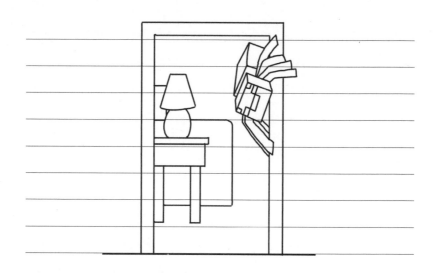

Then I realized Andrew wasn't eating either, because Ziggy was making weird faces at him. Andrew looked miserable—all sniffly and goopy. Maybe his allergies were like my itching. The more stressed out we were, the worse things got.

Then I saw that Cate and Chloe weren't eating either—maybe because this was their first dinner with zombies, and they were disgusted by all the chunks of food spraying out of those gaping zombie mouths. Me? I'm used to that. I sit by Ziggy every day at lunch. But Cate's face was especially green. She looked like she was about to hurl.

Mom kept pushing the food bowls closer, trying to get us all to eat. But even Mom looked grossed out when Mrs. Zombie started picking at a scab on her cheek, right there at the table.

As for Dad? He and Mr. Zombie were having a good old time—chomping away at those chops. In fact, they cleared the chops right off the plate. When Mrs. Zombie asked for more, they were all gone. And Mom looked mortified.

Then Leggy got too close to the table—WAY too close. Like, I saw one of his legs reach for a chunk of potato on MY plate.

I'm not gonna say I screamed, but I might have jumped a little. And for some reason, my baby sister Cammy thought that was hilarious.

She started laughing. Then Zoe the baby zombie started laughing. Then Cammy laughed harder. Then Zoe laughed harder. And then, before anyone could stop her, Cammy blew sky high. The Exploding Baby is the only creeper I know who blows up when she's HAPPY.

BOOM!!!

Gunpowder floated down like snowflakes, all over Mom's "perfect" dinner. And, well, that was the end of that.

Mom practically shoved our guests out the door so that she could clean up the kitchen—or go have a good cry or something.

The good news is, I don't think we'll be "expanding our social circles" with any more of those awkward dinners. The bad news? Andrew is hiding out in the bedroom. He's under the covers, probably plotting his trip back to Humanville. And who can blame him?

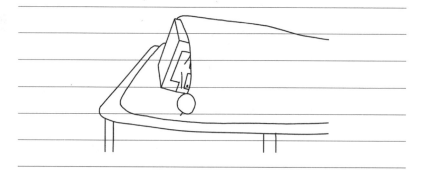

I didn't exactly protect him from Ziggy Zombie. I was too busy protecting myself and my potatoes from Leggy the Spider.

I felt bad for the kid, so I told him through the bed covers that maybe we could start working on that hockey rink tomorrow night, after a good day's sleep. He stopped sniffling for once, so maybe that made him happy.

And now? I'm going to go take a shower and try to stop itching. SHEESH.

DAY 7: MONDAY

Well, I found out what a hockey rink is last night. Or at least how BIG one is. It's as big as our backyard. Yup, we used up every square inch of space—except for a patch of snow-covered grass that Mom said we had to save for Sock the Sheep.

We shoveled the ground flat and then poured out buckets of water, and after HOURS of waiting, that water started to freeze. Then we added more water. And waited for it to freeze. And added more water. And waited.

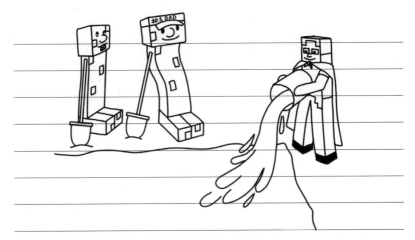

And then Andrew said it was finally thick enough and smooth enough to skate on.

He pulled these things called ice skates out of his trunk. They help him glide across the ice.

Personally, I don't think I need skates. The second I stepped on that ice, I slipped and slid clear across the yard.

I was afraid I was going to fall and break my creeper neck, so I stepped OFF the ice and decided to build a snow golem instead.

But then Andrew said we needed something called "goals." He's got Dad working on them in the garage. I can hear all that sawing and banging right now, when we're supposed to be sleeping.

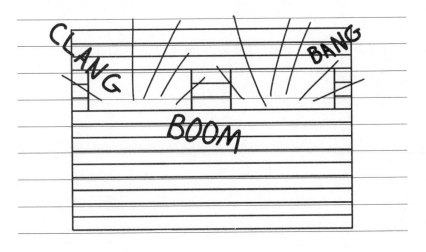

And next to me, Andrew is so stuffy, he's snoring up a storm.

And his glowstone is burning brighter than EVER, like hot lava in the Nether.

I kind of wish it WERE lava, because then it could
burn up that ugly cactus plant sitting beside it.

So now I'm rethinking this hockey thing, and wondering
why I didn't let Andrew just pack his bags last night
and head back to Humanville. I mean, I'm trying to
give the kid a chance—I really am. But this is turning
into an AWFUL lot of work. And I'm SOOOOO tired.

This creeper needs his sleepers, because tomorrow
night?

Drippy and Itchy are heading back to Mob Middle School.

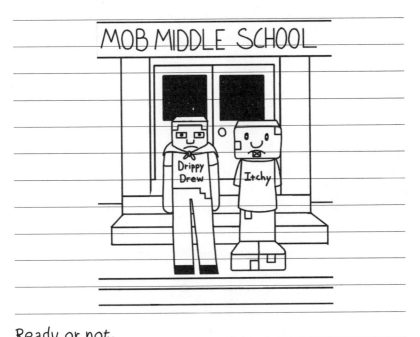

Ready or not.

DAY 8: TUESDAY

"BREAKING NEWS!!! A human steps foot in Mob Middle School!"

That's what Emma Enderman's headline read in the MOB MIDDLE SCHOOL OBSERVER. The paper came out last night, and there were copies of it EVERYWHERE.

A bunch of copies were taped to my locker. When I looked closer at one of them, I saw a giant *photo* of me and Andrew. Well, it was mostly of Andrew. (I was scrunched down so low beside him that Emma had pretty much cut me out of the shot.) And the caption had been scratched out and replaced by "Itchy and Drippy, BFFs." So Bones was at it already.

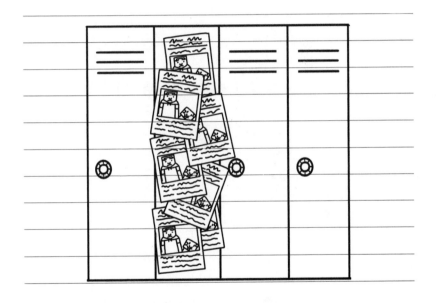

He and *his* buddies had stuffed a bunch of tissues in Drippy's—er, I mean Andrew's—locker. When Andrew opened it, they fluttered out like a colony of white cave bats. He got so nervous, his nose started running, and he actually had to USE one of those tissues.

I started to rip the newspapers off my locker and crumpled them up, but then I decided I'd better read the article. I mean, what if it mentioned ME?

It didn't—not a single word about Gerald Creeper Jr. But Emma sure had a lot to say about Andrew, and between you and me, she KIND of stretched the truth. Read for yourself:

MOB MIDDLE SCHOOL OBSERVER

BREAKING NEWS!!!
A human steps foot in Mob Middle School!

Meet Andrew, a seventh grader who traveled all the way from a farm outside of Humanville to attend our prestigious Mob Middle School.

What does his father do? He mines—even braving the Nether to bring back glowstone souvenirs.

What does his mother do? She farms. Andrew said she grows the biggest pumpkins for miles around! Snow golems, anyone?

Andrew himself is a STAR hockey player back in Humanville. If you don't know what hockey is, ask Andrew. He's planning to organize a game with any mob who wants to learn. Maybe it'll be the NEXT event in the Overworld Games!

At least Emma mentioned hockey. She didn't call Andrew "dude," but she DID make him sound kind of tough, calling him a "star player" and all.

But somehow, I had a bad feeling that newspaper article was going to stir up trouble. And I was right.

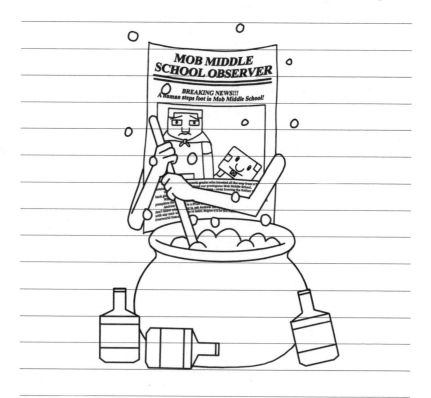

After second period, Andrew and I were walking down the hall. And then suddenly, he wasn't beside me anymore. Some bony fingers had yanked on his cape and pulled him backward.

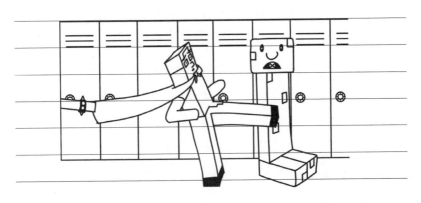

By the time I turned around, a couple of Bones's buddies were dangling Andrew upside down. Then Bones rattled down the hall and said, "So, Drippy, are you challenging the spider jockeys to a game of HOCKEY?"

Aw, crud. This was going nowhere good.

See, Bones and his gang are super competitive. Mostly they compete in Archery and Spider Riding and stuff like that. But I guess when Bones heard some human brag about a new sport in a newspaper article, he felt the urge to challenge him to a game.

I stared at Andrew, sending him warnings with my mind—things like, "Be quiet!" "Don't say a word!" "Don't encourage him!" "Play dead!"

But I guess Andrew didn't get the messages. When he heard "hockey," he got all chatty and told Bones about the rink we had built—in MY backyard. Andrew said it was almost done, that we just had to finish the goals.

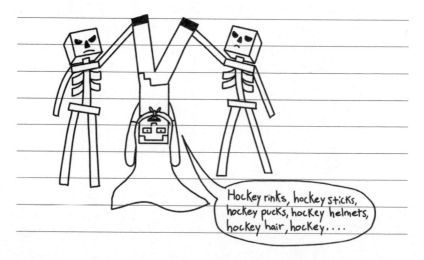

Hockey rinks, hockey sticks, hockey pucks, hockey helmets, hockey hair, hockey....

GREAT.

Bones knew where I lived, and his "friendly little visits" usually ended with something blowing up or being destroyed. So I tried to do some damage control.

"It's not a very big rink," I said. "And my dad probably won't finish those goals for like, I dunno, a month. So, you know, it's no big deal."

"Yeah right, Itchy." Bones flicked me away like a silverfish. Then he turned back to Andrew and said, "Game on, Drippy."

When Bones snapped his bony fingers, his buddies dropped Andrew into a heap on the ground. Then they rattled off to find their next victim.

So . . . that happened. And now I'm going to have to either stall Dad on his goal-making project, or learn to play hockey. FAST.

DAY 9: WEDNESDAY

You know, I once asked Dad to build me an anvil in the garage. It took FOREVER. I think Dad was dragging his feet because the anvil gave him something fun to do. He just didn't WANT the project to end.

But with the hockey goals? The project that I didn't WANT Dad to finish quickly? Dad was done in a flash. OF COURSE.

By the time Andrew and I got home from school this morning, the goals were already set up on the ice. Andrew rushed out back to examine them. "Now we just need nets!" he said. "Something to stop the PUCK from going through the goals."

The WHAT now?

He explained that a puck was like a piece of cobblestone, flint, or coal that you hit through the goals with hockey sticks.

Right away, I suggested spider webs. See, I'm no fan of spiders, but I've become a HUGE fan of spider webs. I once solved a mystery by stretching a spider web across a secret doorway to catch a culprit. But that's a whole other story.

Anyway, I told Andrew that we could get Ziggy's spider to spin us a couple of webs. But as soon as I mentioned Ziggy's name, Andrew turned even more pasty white than he already was. He suggested that maybe we could come up with another idea.

So then I remembered that Mom had a ton of wool that we could use to "weave" webs. It was kind of genius, because it would take a LOT longer than stretching cobwebs across the goals. And I do NOT want those goals to be done too soon.

See, I know that Bones is keeping an eye on this rink. Somehow, he'll know the second that it's finished. And then he'll show up to wipe the ice with me.

So after we got the wool from Mom, I wove my nets as s-l-o-w-l-y as I could. I even broke my wool string a couple of times, just to drag things out. Andrew finished his net before bedtime, but I told him I was going to need another night or two to finish mine—maybe more.

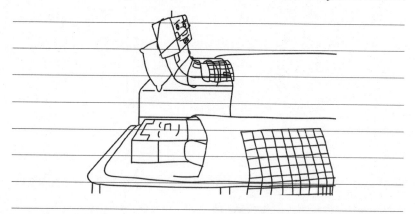

I may not be a star hockey player. But, hey, I'm no dummy either.

DAY 10: THURSDAY

You'd think Mom's dinner with the zombies would have ended her social life—squished it like a silverfish.

SPLAT!

But you know what she said at breakfast this morning? She said she was ready to try ANOTHER dinner party. Maybe with a different mob family this time.

"Cora Creeper's family?" asked Chloe, even though Mom had already told her no on that one. Sometimes my twin isn't the brightest torch on the wall.

But I couldn't help asking again, "Sam and the Slimes?"

Mom ignored us both. "I was thinking about that
nice boy Eddy Enderman. Isn't his mother your
history teacher, Gerald?"

My stomach dropped. I felt like I'd just fallen into
a zombie pit—taken a step without looking and felt
the ground crumble beneath me.

See, I like Eddy Enderman. Who doesn't? He plays
it cool at school. He doesn't try to impress anyone.
He doesn't need to! He just does his own thing, and
shows up every now and then by my side—usually
when I'm stuck between a rock and obsidian and
really need a friend.

So I'm all about hanging out with Eddy. But I'm not sure I want EDDY to hang out with my FAMILY. I mean, my sisters can be SOOO embarrassing!

So I told Mom I was gonna have to think this one through, but . . . she's not really the patient type. I think she's calling Mrs. Enderwoman right now, as I write.

Andrew's not being very patient either. He's outside finishing my goal net FOR me. So much for dragging things out . . . He even got Dad going on making a few extra hockey sticks. I guess you can make them out of old fence posts, which Dad had in his trash heap in the garage.

Throw in a puck made out of coal or cobblestone, and VOILA. We'll have ourselves a hockey game any day now. Ready or not. (SIGH)

DAY 11: FRIDAY

Dad always asks, "What did you learn at school last night?" But the real question is, "What did I learn playing HOCKEY this morning?"

And the answer is, a WHOLE lot. I learned that . . .

* coal flies across the ice way better than flint or cobblestone.

- a SLIME slides across the ice WAY better than a creeper.

- hockey sticks shouldn't be used like swords (even though I might have whacked Sam with mine a time or two "by accident").

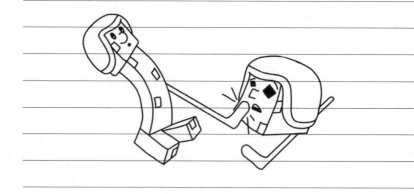

- wool nets are just as sticky as cobwebs (especially when you get tangled up inside one chasing a puck).

- Andrew is WAY less drippy outside than he is when he's inside. And a whole lot tougher.

hockey is not NEARLY as fun as rapping. Andrew can have his hockey stick and puck. I'm sticking to music.

I pretty much made that decision after my first and only try at scoring a goal. Sam was playing goalie, and his wiggly green body filled the WHOLE net, I swear. You can't shoot a goal through a slime's legs. You can't shoot it around him or over him. So finally, I did the only thing I could do. I shot the puck AT him.

And it bounced right off him and flew clear across the rink, landing in MY goal.

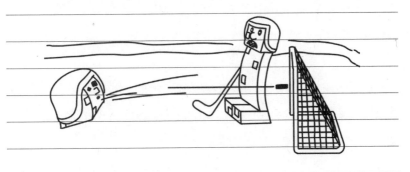

"Own goal!" Andrew shouted. He pumped his fist in the air.

A few seconds later, Sam caught on. "You scored against yourself, Gerald! HA!!!"

Like I hadn't already noticed that my puck had gone into the WRONG net. Thanks, Sam. Thanks for pointing that out, buddy.

When my insides started bubbling over, I made like a puck and flew off the ice.

Then Andrew said I couldn't quit, because he wouldn't have enough players. And I said, "Well, why don't you ask your friend ZIGGY to play?" (I know—that was lame. I didn't say I was PROUD of it.)

That's when Chloe came out of the house and grabbed my stick. She'd probably been waiting all morning to take my place.

I almost stuck around to watch her play. But if I had, Chloe probably would have scored like a gazillion goals and made it look EASY. My Evil Twin has a way of kicking me when I'm down—making a miserable creeper feel even worse.

So I marched back to my room. For once, I had it all to myself. I threw a blanket over Andrew's glowstone—and the poky cactus plant. And when I caught Sticky gazing toward the door, waiting for Andrew, I threw a blanket over his aquarium, too. I mean, the squid is kind of a traitor for getting all attached to a HUMAN when he already has a perfectly loyal creeper boy, right?

Then I did what I always do when I feel miserable. I rapped.

I think a hockey puck just hit my bedroom window. (Thank you, Chloe.) But I'm not going back out there. Not even if Bones himself comes rapping on my window, daring me to show him what I've got.

Let Chloe take on Bones for all I care. I'm done defending Andrew. With a hockey stick in his hands, the kid can defend himself.

DAY 12: SATURDAY

So when I woke up for school last night, I was
feeling much better (thanks for asking). I even
reread my last journal entry and thought I MIGHT
have overreacted. (Mom says I can be kind of
dramatic sometimes.)

But then I went to school. And Sam let it slip to
his girlfriend Willow Witch that the hockey rink was

done. And that means EVERYONE at Mob Middle School will know by Monday, if not before. Emma Enderman will probably even publish an update in the paper: "THE GAME IS ON!"

So I've got to either magically learn how to play hockey this weekend, or run for the hills before Bones and his buddies show up for a game.

I'm thinking it might be time to take another look at my 30-Day Plan.

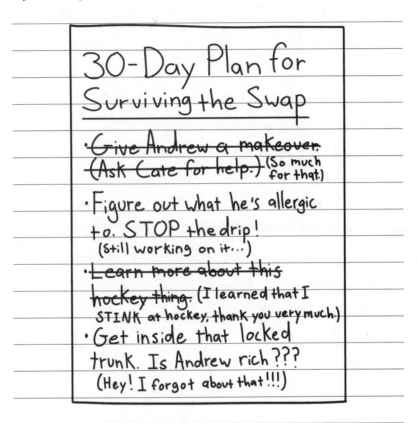

30-Day Plan for
Surviving the Swap

• ~~Give Andrew a makeover.~~
~~(Ask Cate for help.)~~ (So much for that.)

• Figure out what he's allergic to. STOP the drip!
(Still working on it...)

• ~~Learn more about this~~
~~hockey thing.~~ (I learned that I STINK at hockey, thank you very much.)

• Get inside that locked trunk. Is Andrew rich ???
(Hey! I forgot about that !!!)

See, it's good to dust off the plan every now and then, because I TOTALLY forgot about the trunk. If there really is some kind of treasure in there, I MIGHT not have to run for the hills. Or play hockey. EVER. Andrew and I can just fling a few diamonds or emeralds in Bones's direction in exchange for a little peace. Or we can buy Andrew a one-way ticket back to Humanville. Something like that.

Either way, I gotta get into that trunk, because a creeper's gotta keep his options open.

It just hit me that I had the PERFECT chance to break into the trunk yesterday morning, when I was alone in my room. But instead? I pouted and felt all sorry for myself. I mean, I did get a good rap song out of the deal, but still . . .

Andrew is already out playing hockey with Chloe, so maybe I can find something to use to pick the lock RIGHT NOW. I'll be back in a sec!

CURSES!!! Mom caught me snooping in the drawer for one of Cammy's baby forks, and I got roped into helping her clean the house. I totally forgot the Endermans are coming over tonight. So . . . my lock-picking is going to have to wait.

Stay tuned . . .

DAY 13: SUNDAY

Sure, scoring an "own goal" in hockey is
embarrassing. But having Eddy Enderman meet my
family was downright MORTIFYING.

Every single thing I worried about CAME TRUE. And
even a few things I didn't see coming . . .

First of all, before dinner, Cate told Andrew NOT
to look the Endermans in the eye. It's just kind
of a thing with them, she said—it makes them
uncomfortable, and sometimes they get downright
salty about it.

But Dad overheard and took the whole "don't look
an Enderman in the eye" thing to a whole new level.
When we sat down at the dinner table, Dad tried
passing the potatoes to Mrs. Enderwoman without
looking at her—and ended up tossing those tots
right in her lap. GREAT start to the night, Dad. Thank
you very much.

Then Chloe started yammering, asking Mrs. Enderwoman about the history of the Overworld. She said, "Since you TEACH history, Mrs. Enderwoman, maybe you could settle an argument between my dad and Andrew."

An ARGUMENT? That was kind of an exaggeration, if you ask me.

But Dad got all into it. He told Mrs. Enderwoman HIS version of the history of the Overworld—you know, where mobs were here before humans. And then Andrew kind of whispered his version (because I think he was freaked out by the Endermen at the table). And then Chloe stared hard at Mrs. Enderwoman and said, "SO, who's RIGHT?"

I caught Eddy's eye—I'm not afraid to do that anymore—and rolled my own eyes. I wanted to remind him that I'm NOT related to Chloe by CHOICE. But he just smiled and played it cool. No surprise there.

Then Mrs. Enderwoman said politely that none of us REALLY know how things went down so long ago. And Mom backed her up by changing the subject.

But Chloe would NOT let go of this history thing. She was like a wolf-dog with a bone. "Was Herobrine

the first human to walk the Overworld?" she asked
Mrs. Enderwoman.

I almost choked on my chop.

See, Herobrine is supposed to be the ghost of
a dead miner—a HUMAN miner—who stalks the
Overworld. He has glowing white eyes and a crooked,
twitchy head. He'd be super scary—and maybe even
an interesting thing to talk about at dinner—except
for ONE problem: Herobrine is NOT REAL. Everyone
knows that! Everyone except Chloe, apparently.
No matter how many times I try to shut down the
Herobrine thing, she brings it right back up.

"Herobrine is FAKE!" I said as I fake-coughed.

Chloe heard me loud and clear and kicked me under the table.

"Herobrine is just a legend, dear," agreed Mrs. Enderwoman. "Could you please pass the carrots?"

Chloe passed the carrots. Then she tried again. "What do you think, Andrew?" she asked. "Have you ever seen Herobrine?"

Andrew shook his head and then blew his nose.
Twice. Maybe he was hoping Chloe would take the
hint and back off.

But she didn't. "Haven't you seen the signs,
Andrew?" she said. "Trees with no leaves . . ."

Andrew fiddled with his carrots.

"Um, yeah, Chloe—it's winter," I pointed out.
"There aren't leaves on ANY trees."

"How about random glowstone towers?" she said,
ignoring me. "Herobrine likes to build glowstone
towers, you know."

Well, that kind of made me think. I mean, Andrew
DOES love his glowstone. Could *he* be related to
the legendary human Herobrine? I snuck a peek at
Andrew, who was sinking lower in his chair.

But Chloe wasn't finished yet. "Herobrine can even
take control of ANIMALS," she said, her voice rising.
"Make *them* do exactly what he wants them to do!"

Now my pork chop WAS stuck in my throat. And I
couldn't even look at Andrew. Because, I mean, he
DOES have a way with animals. Maybe he had Sticky
UNDER HIS CONTROL. Maybe Andrew was *possessed*
by the ghost of Herobrine!

"And he catches mobs in traps, too," said Chloe, narrowing her eyes at me. "Herobrine sets traps for mobs like us so that he can steal our things."

When I actually started choking, Eddy teleported beside me in a flash and whacked my back. A hunk of meat flew across the table and landed on Cammy's plate.

Chloe wrinkled her nose as if I were the grossest mob ever. But Cammy? Well, she started laughing. Hard. And, well, you know what happened next.

<u>Yup. Ka-BOOM!</u>

Mrs. Enderwoman teleported away from the table, nearly knocking over a cactus plant. Then she said they had to get home to, um, let the dog out or something. Poor Mom, who was covered in gunpowder, offered to send a pork chop home for Pearl, Eddy's wolf-dog.

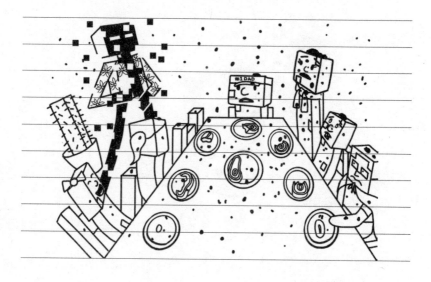

But Eddy said Pearl only eats SKELETON bones.

See? This is why I like Eddy Enderman. Bones and his spider jockey friends don't mess with Eddy. Why would they? His wolf-dog could take them down in a single hungry chomp.

On the way out the door, Eddy said, "See you Monday, Gerald. See ya, Andrew. Maybe I can try out your hockey rink this week."

Um, WHAT now? Eddy KNEW about our hockey rink? And wanted to play???

I didn't know if I should be thrilled or horrified. I mean, I prefer to have Eddy see me at my BEST—not face-planting across the ice and sliding straight into my own goal.

So before Andrew and Eddy could sync up their calendars and pick a hockey date, I shoved Eddy out the door and waved goodbye to Mrs. Enderwoman. Then I helped Mom sweep up the gunpowder.

I gotta say, though, I kept a pretty close eye on Andrew for the rest of the night. Because all that stuff Chloe said about Herobrine started getting under my skin, and I was feeling pretty itchy. Itchy to know more about my boy Andrew.

Itchy to figure out what was in that trunk.

DAY 15: TUESDAY

Did I mention I hate Mondays?

Yeah, I'd be good with a six-night week. Sure, it would mean 52 fewer nights a year, but if they're all school nights, I'd cheerfully give them up. Just saying . . .

September						
Sun	Mon	Tue	wed	Thu	Fri	Sat
1	2	3	4	5	6	7
8	9	10	11	12	13	14
	16	17	18	19	20	21
22		24	25	26	27	28
29	30					

See, Monday night started with a BANG. Not the kind you hear when Cammy explodes or anything like that. It was more like the lid of Andrew's treasure chest slamming down on my NOSE.

Andrew had actually left the chest UNLOCKED while he grabbed a shower. I didn't notice till I happened to casually creep by and nudge the lid with my toe. And sure enough, it opened! So I practically dove into that trunk to see what was in there. And that was the exact second Andrew flew back into the room and slammed the lid.

OUCH!!!

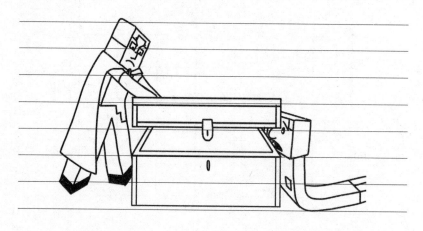

My nose swelled up like a pufferfish, and Andrew didn't even APOLOGIZE. He was all like, "What are you LOOKING for in there?" and I was like, "I dunno. What are you HIDING in there?" And that's how we ended up giving each other the silent treatment all the way to school.

Except Chloe wasn't silent. My Evil Twin had figured out that talking about Herobrine made Andrew REALLY uncomfortable. So of course, she babbled on about it while we walked.

She pointed out all the trees that had no leaves. She actually spotted a glowstone tower near the swamp—a random tower that I've NEVER seen before that actually DID kind of pop up overnight. And when we passed a stray cat, Chloe said, "Don't you want to tame it, Andrew, and take

it home? I mean, you're good at that—you and
Herobrine."

Normally, I'd tell Chloe to shut it. But my nose was
throbbing from being slammed in that chest—proof
that Andrew DID have something to hide. So I let
him take the heat from Chloe all the way to school.
And I watched him carefully, waiting for him to crack
and let something slip.

Then Sam bounced over and said he had GREAT news—that LOTS of mobs wanted to play hockey with us, now that our rink was finished.

It's like the slime had completely forgotten about the last time we'd played hockey. Did he think I'd be EXCITED about another game? Sheesh. He might as well have socked me in my swollen nose while he was at it. With a best friend like Sam, who needs enemies?

Andrew suddenly quit with the silent treatment and got all chatty with Sam. They started talking about having the game Saturday night. By lunchtime, they had a bunch of mobs signed up to play. And by the end of the school night, Bones was all up in my face about the game.

"You're going DOWN, Itchy," he said, flicking my nose with his bony finger.

I would have hissed out the perfect comeback, I'm sure. Except my nose stung so bad that my eyes got all watery. And a creeper does NOT shed tears in front of a spider jockey. Not a single drop. EVER.

So instead, I made like an Enderman and "teleported" home as fast as I could. And then I MIGHT have shed a tear or two, but only because holding all that water in was making my nose throb.

Every time I look at that locked chest in my room, I start to hiss. If I were even the TINIEST bit like my Evil Twin, I'd just blow my fuse and blast my way into that chest. But I'm not really that kind of creeper.

Dad says I use my brains, not my blasts—like my Great-Great Grandpa Gerald. But I gotta say, my brains are tired from working overtime. And my nose hurts. And all I really want to do right now is RAP.

Okay, the front door just creaked open, which means Andrew's back from school. Which means rap time is OVER.

Time to put my game face back on.

DAY 17: THURSDAY

Dad says it's okay to toot your own horn when you do something genius. I think the old man has a point there. I mean, if you don't cheer for yourself, who else is going to?

So here's what I did:

I hit the school library looking for answers. Not the kind you find at the end of Sherlock Bones or Agatha Crispy mysteries. And DEFINITELY not the kind of answers you find in those "facts of life" books, like the one I accidentally checked out last fall. (I'm still having nightmares about some of those pictures.)

No, I went into the library looking for a way OUT of the hockey game. See, everything I know about hockey, I learned from Andrew. And I'm starting to wonder if hockey is just one big trap he's setting for me—to make me look bad. Or to make himself look good. Or to prove that humans are BETTER than other mobs.

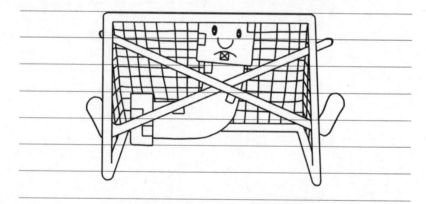

So if I can research hockey, I might be able to figure out a new angle here. A way to beat Andrew at his own game.

Mrs. Collins was in the library, and she's always THRILLED to see me walk through the door. She was all like, "Hello, Gerald. How nice to see you! What can I do for you today?"

Since she offered, I put her to work right away— digging up facts on this human extracurricular called "hockey." She didn't have a ton of books, but the one she DID have was very useful, I gotta say. It was full of pictures of hockey players.

When I studied those pictures, I saw that one guy was wearing his own kind of uniform. It had these stripes on it. (He kind of looked like my not-so-Great Uncle who blew up the village well and had to go to jail. I saw his mug shot in an old copy of the Creeper Chronicle. But that's a whole other story.)

Anyway, the guy in the stripes is called a "referee." And HE's the guy with all the power. He starts the game, and gives penalties to players who break the rules, and decides whether a goal is actually scored. And here's the BEST part: He DOESN'T have to play!

So I'm thinking this referee job is PERFECT for me. I memorized every rule in that book. Yup, I know more about refereeing a hockey game than Andrew will EVER know. And I have the perfect striped sweater to wear for the job, thanks to Mom and her knitting needles.

So like I said, I tooted my own horn all the way home this morning. And now? I can't WAIT for Saturday night's game.

BRING IT ON.

DAY 19: SATURDAY MORNING

There's a reason I can't cut Mondays from the calendar. Why? Because Mom won't let me.

See, parents control calendars. A creep can't make a single plan for himself without running it past Mom first.

Like the hockey game, for example. It's happening tonight. Every mob at school KNOWS about it and is planning on it. But I made the mistake of NOT letting Mom know about the game. (Well, actually, ANDREW made that mistake.) And it turns out, she made other plans for us.

She told me at dinner last night that we're having another dinner party tonight.

SERIOUSLY???

You'd think Mom would have learned her lesson after the first two. This mob-mixing thing just doesn't really work. But she said she has extra special guests coming, and that it's a surprise, and that Andrew and I had better have our butts at the table—or else.

So I had to send out a news alert through Emma Enderman at school last night that the hockey game might start a TAD later than planned. It'd be more of an "after dinner" kind of thing.

Hopefully, everyone got the memo. Otherwise, Mom's going to have to set a few more places at the dinner table.

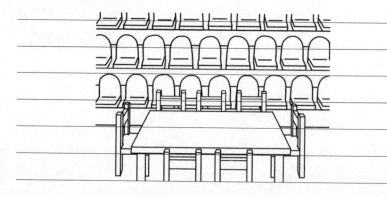

DAY 19: SATURDAY NIGHT

Parents are CLUELESS. Like, even if clues came POURING out of the sky, my parents wouldn't catch any of them. If someone was handing out clues in the street for free, my mom would be like, "Ah, no thanks. We don't need any."

So guess who Mom invited over for dinner tonight. No, really: GUESS.

Not creepers or zombies or Endermen. Not witches or slimes or zombie pigmen. Not pigs or chickens or horses. No, not even HUMANS.

She invited SKELETONS. And not just any skeletons. Oh, no—when Mom messes up, her mistakes are EPIC. She goes all the way.

Mom invited BONES and his dad to dinner.

My special "surprise" was the biggest bully at Mob Middle School sitting next to me at my own dinner table.

I guess Bones's dad works with MY dad, and they got to talking one day and realized that Bones and I were going to the same school, and one thing led to another, and . . . well, you can't make this stuff up.

Bones looked as surprised as I did when he walked through the door, at least for a second. But during dinner, he got that gaping grin, and his bony fingers started twitching—like he couldn't WAIT to use this opportunity to really stick it to me.

And after what had happened at the last two dinners, I knew my family would give _him_ PLENTY of ammunition.

After dinner, Mom was like, "Gerald, why don't you and Andrew take Bones into your room to play?" She actually said that—"to PLAY." Like we were going to bust out Cammy's creeper dolls and have a tea party or something.

"Mom, we've got a hockey game," I reminded her—in my toughest, growliest voice.

Then she said I'd better remember to "wear a sweater and my thermal underwear." GREAT.

Now let me get one thing straight: creepers do NOT wear underwear. But when Mom was on her knitting kick, she knit all KINDS of things that this creeper would never be caught dead in.

So the second we got to the bedroom, Bones started in. He saw the glowstone on the dresser and was like, "Aw, what a cute little LIGHT. Do Itchy and Drippy need to keep a light on during the day so they can SLEEP?"

I started to hiss. When Bones flicked his finger against Sticky's aquarium, I knew I had to do something—fast.

"Can I get some privacy here?" I said, grabbing my sweater and pushing Bones and Andrew back out the door.

"You gotta put on your thermal UNDIES, Gerald?" crooned Bones.

I'm pretty sure I saw Andrew's mouth twitch, like he actually thought that was FUNNY. Well, Drippy Drew and Bones could buddy up all they wanted. I was DONE.

I slammed the door so hard after them, the water in Sticky's aquarium sloshed from side to side.

Now I'm re-reading my plan and trying not to blow.

I'M IN CHARGE, I keep reminding myself. I'M the referee. I'M the one who can kick players out of the game if they break rules. I'M the one who decides if a goal counts or not. So I'M the one who decides who wins.

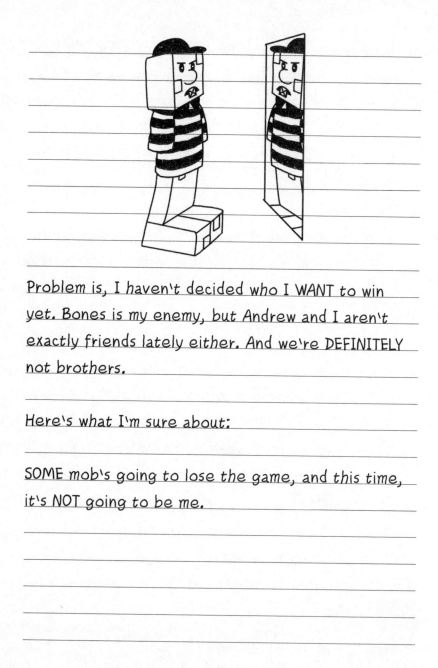

Problem is, I haven't decided who I WANT to win yet. Bones is my enemy, but Andrew and I aren't exactly friends lately either. And we're DEFINITELY not brothers.

Here's what I'm sure about:

SOME mob's going to lose the game, and this time, it's NOT going to be me.

DAY 20: SUNDAY MORNING

Don't. Even. Ask.

I don't want to talk about it.

I mean, we could talk about how UNFAIR life is. Like how referees are SUPPOSED to have power, but they really don't—not when every mob on the ice gangs up on them.

Or like how much it stinks when mobs that are SUPPOSED to be your friends, like zombies and slimes and Endermen, decide to team up with the human

141

who has been making your life miserable for the last three weeks.

Or like how even when a creeper decides NOT TO PLAY hockey, he can still somehow take a puck to the face. And get a swollen lip. And start talking with a lisp.

But, hey, if we're going to talk about all THAT, I might as well just tell you how the game went— before I block it permanently from my memory.

Here goes:

- I started the game with a faceoff. Bones and Andrew came to the middle of the rink, and I dropped the coal between their sticks. Andrew hit the coal toward the goal. Bones whacked ME in the leg.

- Andrew passed to Chloe, then Eddy teleported to the goal and caught the pass from Chloe. One of Bones's spider jock friends elbowed Eddy, and

I called a *penalty*. LOUD. But every single mob on the ice ignored me.

- Bones took the coal down the ice toward the other goal, which Sam was *pretty much* filling out with his ginormous green body. When the coal bounced off Sam, everyone cheered for Sam. Except me. Because my nose hurt just THINKING about the last time I'd seen a puck bounce off Sam.

- Ziggy took the coal down the ice, and Bones pulled his sword—er, stick—on Ziggy. "Slashing!" I called out. But no one listened. "Spearing!" I shouted. Nothing. "Tripping!" That last one was kind of a stretch, but I mean, Ziggy DID kind of stagger when Bones hit him with his stick.

- Bones turned on me and shouted something I CAN'T repeat. "Misconduct!" I shouted. "Go to the penalty box!" The penalty box was Sock the Sheep's pen. But it might have been in the Nether, for all Bones cared, because he WASN'T GOING.

- Bones stole the puck from Ziggy, skated toward me, and took a slap shot.

- I took a _hundred-mile-per-hour puck to the pie hole._

- I _spit out blood and kicked Bones out of the game._

- Bones raised *his bony hand to his ear* and said, "What's that, Lispy? I can't understand you!"

- Chloe burst out laughing.

- The game went on WITHOUT me. And no one—not my sister, or my best friend, Sam, or my sort-of friend Ziggy, or my coolest friend, Eddy—came to see if I was alright. Or backed me up. Or ANYTHING.

They're still playing out there, and I'm sitting in my room hissing mad.

There's only one mob to blame for all this.

And _he's_ not even a mob.

ANDREW.

I TRIED to help him fit in at Mob Middle School—with a makeover and a nickname. I tried to make him less drippy, by figuring out what he was allergic to. I even helped him build his dumb hockey rink so that Bones would think he was tough and maybe show the dude some respect. And what did Andrew do to THANK me?

He moved into my house, into my room, into my LIFE—and took it all over. He took control of my room with his annoying glowstone. He took control of my squid with his Herobrine powers. He took control of my BEST friends and my BACKYARD and even my FACE with his crummy hockey pucks.

And now I'm not hissing mad, I'm BOILING mad. Hot lava is spitting and popping inside me. I'm going to BLOW—I can FEEL it.

Any. Second. Now.

DAY 20: SUNDAY NIGHT

I'm a peaceful creeper.

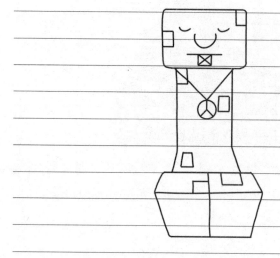

I use my brains more than my blasts.

At least that's what I've been telling myself my WHOLE creeper life. And it's what I've been telling Andrew all day, too. But he won't listen.

Maybe it's because everything he owns is covered in gunpowder. Or because his glowstone was blown to smithereens. Or because his treasure chest was blown wide open.

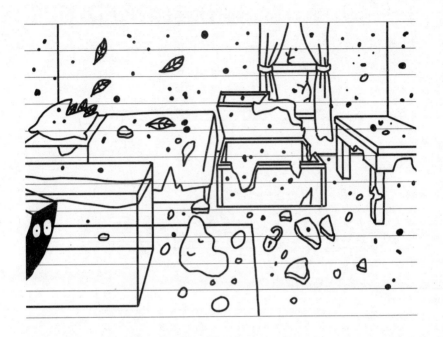

For days now, I've been dying to know what was in there. And now? I wish I'd never looked. I wish I could just rewind to the start of this whole Mob School Swap and do it all over again. Do it differently this time. Do it like Great-Great-Grandpa Gerald would have.

But I'll never get that chance.

There wasn't a speck of treasure in that chest. No diamonds. No emeralds. No weapons. No armor. Just some lousy seeds to remind Andrew of the farm he lives on. And a newspaper article.

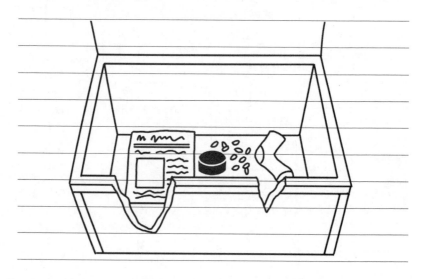

The article was so old and yellow that I'm surprised it didn't catch fire with my explosion. But when the lid to that chest blew open, there was the article, folded neatly in the bottom of the trunk, staring me in the face.

Great-Great-Grandpa GERALD was staring me in the face. The article showed a photo of him, with a caption that read "Creeper extends invitation of peace and hospitality to humans."

Dad showed me that article before. It's all about
the first Overworld Games, which Great-Great-
Grandpa Gerald organized to bring different kinds
of mobs—and even humans—together for a friendly,
peaceful competition.

Like I said, Great-Great-Grandpa Gerald was all
about peace. He was a vegetarian who raised pigs
for riding, not eating. He recycled gunpowder to
make fireworks. And he volunteered to rebuild
houses that OTHER creepers had blown apart. I'm
sure there were LOTS of newspaper articles written
about my great-great-grandpa.

But why did ANDREW have one of them in his chest?
Was this some kind of JOKE?

Turns out, the only joke was on me.

When Andrew saw what I'd done to his things,
he started to blubber all over them. (I think the
gunpowder was messing with his allergies.) He said
that newspaper article was the WHOLE reason he had
come to our house. His parents had seen the article
and thought that if we were related to Great-Great-
Grandpa Gerald, we would be peaceful creepers who
would be nice to Andrew and make him feel welcome.

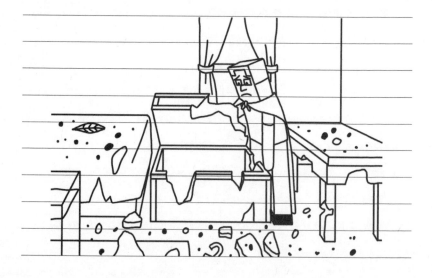

"Well, why didn't you TELL me that?" I hissed. I mean, it might have been a good thing for me to know.

Andrew said he had TRIED to tell me that first night over dinner. "I thought you'd all be vegetarians like your grandpa!" said Andrew. "But you acted all weird about me not eating pork chops. SNIFF, SNIFFLE. So I figured that maybe you WEREN'T like your grandpa. SNIFF, SNIFF. And maybe you wouldn't appreciate me bringing him up. SNORT."

Andrew wiped his nose and said a few more things, but all I heard was my conscience saying, "You're a loser, Gerald. You're a loser, Gerald. You're a LOSER!"

Because I had not only let Andrew down. I had let Great-Great-Grandpa GERALD down. My namesake— the relative that my dad always says I'm the MOST like.

Well, so much for that. I hadn't been nice to Andrew. Or made him feel welcome. I mean, I did at FIRST—but only till the going got tough for me. Then I pretty much threw Andrew to the wolves (or at least to the spider jockeys).

So now I'm spending the whole night "thinking about what I did." Mom grounded me, but she didn't even have to. I feel too lousy to want to leave my room anyway—even though the only things that survived my blow-up were Sticky's aquarium and that CRUMMY cactus plant.

Sticky is giving me the stink-eye, as if I didn't feel guilty enough. HE was nice to Andrew. HE was welcoming. Even STICKY acted more like Great-Great-Grandpa Gerald than I did.

So I dunno. Maybe I'll end up getting kicked out of the Creeper Family Tree.

And you know what?

I'll deserve it.

DAY 22: TUESDAY MORNING

So Andrew's the new hero of Mob Middle School.

Turns out, his team beat Bones and the spider jockeys in the hockey game Saturday night. I hadn't even bothered to ask. (I guess I was too busy blowing up my room and all of my Overworldly possessions, plus a few of Andrew's, too.)

But I know something that Andrew doesn't: Bones NEVER gives up. If he wants to take Andrew down, he WILL. One way or another.

So I want to tell Andrew to watch his back. But why would he listen to a thing this creeper has to say? He and Sam are hanging out now. Andrew is even looking pretty chummy with Ziggy. I guess they bonded over hockey or something. And they're actually talking about playing ANOTHER hockey game this weekend.

But I won't be refereeing that one. Nope. I'll just be watching from the shadows like a zombie-wannabe who doesn't really belong. Hand me a rotten-flesh sandwich, why don't you, because I'm pretty sure being a zombie would feel better right now than being Gerald Creeper Jr.

SIGH.

DAY 24: THURSDAY MORNING

Here's the thing about being like a zombie:

When everyone ignores you, you hear a lot of things that no one KNOWS you heard. Like, you hear that there's going to be a sleepover after the next hockey game, maybe at your very own house. Even though you weren't officially invited.

And you hear that a certain group of skeletons might not only terrorize your friends (EX-friends?) during that game, but that they might crash the sleepover afterward. And totally destroy it. You hear details—things like "flaming arrows" and "spiders." Those bony bullies do NOT mess around.

And you TRY to tell your friends what you heard. But when you're a zombie, NOBODY listens.

"Andrew," I said for the third time after school this morning. "You gotta cancel the hockey game. Bones and his friends are going to play rough. Someone's going to get HURT."

But he just stared at me, sniffling. And he finally said, "If you want to play, Gerald, just PLAY. No one's stopping you."

SHEESH.

You try to help a guy out, and he turns it around and thinks it's all about YOU.

So I said to Chloe, "Get Mom and Dad to cancel the sleepover this weekend. Bones and his gang of bullies are going to crash it. Do NOT let that sleepover happen."

But Chloe's eyes lit up. See, that girl never backs down from a challenge—or a fight. "Let them crash it," she hissed, sounding almost EXCITED about the opportunity.

So I went to my parents. And trust me, that's usually my LAST option. I am NOT the kind of guy who goes around ratting out his friends—or enemies. But it felt like a giant snowball was rolling toward my house, and I was the ONLY one who could see it. The only one who could STOP it!

"Mom," I said before breakfast. "Andrew wants to have another hockey game, but I know for a fact it's going to end in DISASTER. Can you put the kibosh on it? PLEASE?"

But she just looked at me with those sad Mom eyes and said, "Gerald, you and Andrew really need to make up. Just tell him you're sorry."

SERIOUSLY???

So I went to Dad. Every once in a while, the old guy comes through for me.

This was NOT one of those times.

After I made my case, he grabbed a hockey stick and said, "You just need to build your confidence, son. C'mon. Let's hit the ice."

ARGH!!!!!!!!!!!

The LAST thing I need right now is to have my DAD giving me hockey lessons. I might have said those exact words before storming out of the garage in a huff.

So, I give up. I did EVERYTHING I could do to try to protect Andrew this time. And no one listened to a word I had to hiss.

WHATEVS. Not my problem.

Let the coal chips fall where they may (as Mom likes to say).

DAY 24: THURSDAY MORNING (AGAIN)

I. Can't. Sleep.

I keep putting down my pencil, but it keeps hopping right back up—like it's BEGGING me to come up with a plan.

But I HAD a plan. A plan to make Andrew look cooler and tougher so that mobs at middle school wouldn't eat him alive. A plan to get inside that trunk and learn more about Andrew—to find SOMETHING that would make Bones and his buddies RESPECT Andrew.

And none of it worked!

So what do you want me to do, Mr. Pencil? HUH,
tough guy? Tell me!!!

WAKE UP, YA
LAZY CREEPER!
WE NEED A
PLAN!

DAY 24: THURSDAY NIGHT

Sheesh. Be careful what you wish for.

I finally DID fall asleep, and I had the WORST daymare (thanks to my sister Chloe).

Herobrine was gliding toward me, and that dude is SCARY. I saw his eyes first, glowing like an ocelot's. Then I saw the twitch, twitch, twitch of his crooked head. But as he got closer . . . close enough to almost GRAB me . . . I saw that it wasn't Herobrine at all.

It was ANDREW.

I _must_ have woken up hollering, because Andrew ran over to see what was wrong. But seeing HIS face scared me even more. Were his eyes glowing? Did his head look crooked—maybe just a little?

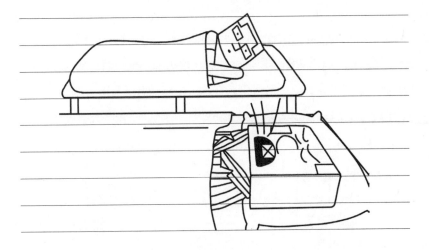

YIKES. I'll never look at Andrew the same way again, let me tell you. If Bones and his gang had seen what I just saw in my dream, THEY wouldn't mess with Andrew again either.

The dude doesn't need a hockey stick or a chest full of treasure. He's got HEROBRINE on his side.

DAY 26: SATURDAY

Well, I tried to warn them—all of them.

But they're out there in the backyard RIGHT NOW, playing hockey. I mean, if you can call it "playing."

Bones showed up riding a SPIDER. And his buddies are carrying SWORDS instead of hockey sticks. So that ice looks a lot more like a battlefield than a hockey rink.

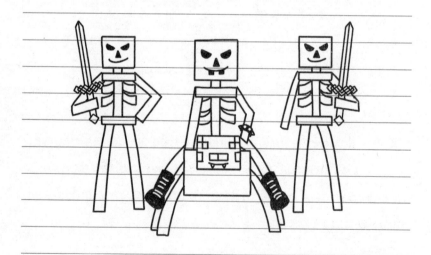

And even though I know it's not going to be pretty, I can't look away.

Bones is taking the puck down the ice with his sword. No one's trying to stop him—I mean, WHO would? Even Sam bounced right out of the goal when he saw Bones coming with that sword. Score one for the spider jock.

Andrew's got the puck now, but guess who's playing goalie for the skeletons? A SPIDER.

Andrew's usually pretty good with critters, but that red-eyed beast in front of the goal is making Andrew sweat, I can tell. Just looking at that hairy-legged monster is making ME sweat. And itch.

The spider just tripped Andrew with one of its hairy legs. Now he's pulling him toward the goal!!!

I. Can't. Look.

Should I go out there? Get Dad involved? I DON'T KNOW WHAT TO DO!!!

Okay, Andrew made it out of that mess alive. PHEW!!!

And I'm going to keep recording all of this so that if my friends perish, I can tell the world what happened. I'll write a newspaper article that people will HAVE to read. I'll cut out the article and send it back to Andrew's parents in his wooden trunk. I'll sniffle and say, "I'm sorry about your son. He was a good one."

Okay, I just took another peek out the window. Chloe is all up in Bones's face right now. Leave it to my sister to take a stand, even when she doesn't stand a chance.

I think I can hear her hissing.

Yup, that's definitely hissing.

I know what happens next.

BOOM!!!!!!

It's snowing outside my window right now, except that's not snow—it's gunpowder and shards of ice. CLINK, CLINK, CLINK. Andrew's precious hockey rink just got blown into a gazillion pieces.

It's awfully quiet out there now.

I just looked, and it's not pretty.

Bones and his spider are taking a victory lap around what USED to be a hockey rink. Sam is a green puddle of sadness. Ziggy is staggering around like he doesn't know what happened. But . . . where's Andrew?

There he is—sitting in the penalty box (Sock the Sheep's pen). I guess Andrew is giving himself a time out.

He looks so LITTLE out there, slumped over his broken hockey stick. I'm pretty sure I just saw him wipe his nose on his sleeve, poor drippy kid. I want to shout at him, "GET UP! BLOW YOUR NOSE! DON'T GIVE UP!"

But the game is over. Done. Kaput.

And the sleepover? Well, Bones is probably rubbing his bony hands together right now, perfecting his evil plan to wreck that, too. And I can't do a thing to stop it.

Where's the ghost of Herobrine when you need him?

I can see it all in my mind—Andrew rising up, larger than life, and staggering toward Bones with his twitchy head and glowing white eyes. Bones would be so spooked, he'd fall right off his disgusting spider. I'd pay good emeralds to see THAT.

But like I keep telling Chloe, Herobrine's not real. He's not coming to save the day.

UNLESS . . .

Oh, man. When you're a brainiac like me, Gerald Creeper Jr., you never know when genius is gonna strike.

Genius

I'd tell you my idea, but there's no time. I gotta go find the one creeper who can help me pull this off:

CATE.

DAY 27: SUNDAY

You know what?

I think if Great-Great-Grandpa Gerald could have seen what went down today, he'd be proud of me.

It was a pretty sorry bunch of mobs who stayed for the sleepover this morning. Andrew was so bummed about the hockey rink that he was especially drippy. The kid didn't even bother to wipe his nose anymore. He just let it run.

Sam was as flat as a pancake. And Ziggy didn't even have the energy to pick at his scabs and blisters.

Until I told them my plan.

See, I knew Bones was going to show up at the break of dawn to ruin the sleepover. And I figured we could all just sit here like mushrooms on a log, or we could take action.

So here's what went down:

Bones showed up, alright. I heard the scratch of his long, yellow fingernail across my windowpane. Now, normally that would have freaked me out. But today? I was ready.

Sam and Ziggy could have won awards for their acting, too. We all crept outside, pretending like we were "investigating" the source of the scratching noise.

"Is it Herobrine?" I hissed to Sam—super loud like.

He wiggled and jiggled as if he really WERE scared. "I d-d-d-dunno," he said. "I hope not! Herobrine can take control of our MINDS."

"He's HEEEEERE!" moaned Ziggy, really getting into it. "I can FEEEEEL it!"

That's when Bones jumped out from behind a bush. "HA!!! GOTCHA!!!" He raised his bony fingers in the air and wiggled them. "Oooohhhh, I'm Herobrine, coming to take control of your MINDS! Bah-ha-ha-ha-ha." He slapped his bony hand on his bony thigh, as if we were the saddest, sorriest mobs he'd ever seen.

That's when Andrew made his move.

He floated out of the darkness, glowing like a wither skeleton in the Nether. His eyes were SO white. TWITCH. TWITCH. TWITCH. His head jerked toward his shoulder as he crept toward Bones.

"Aaaaan-drew?" Ziggy moaned. "Is that yooooooou?"

"N-no!" blubbered Sam. "It's the g-ghost of Herobrine!"

"Andrew IS Herobrine!" I shouted.

TWITCH. TWITCH. TWITCH. Andrew kept his glowing eyes trained on Bones and took another step toward him. And then another.

And that's when Bones fell apart.

I never saw that jock look more rattled. His bones shook so loud, I thought they were going to come unhinged. I thought we'd have a whole PILE of bones to give to Pearl, Eddy's wolf-dog.

But somehow, Bones pulled himself together enough to run for the hills. He screeched and squealed all the way.

And that's when Andrew started laughing—we ALL did. And before I knew it, Andrew started looking more like himself again, even with all that white

makeup and the glow-in-the-dark contacts we'd
borrowed from Cate.

So like I said, I think Great-Great-Grandpa Gerald
would be proud. I found a PEACEFUL way to stand
up for Andrew—or to help the dude stand up for
himself.

And it felt a whole lot better than blowing my
bedroom to smithereens.

DAY 30: WEDNESDAY

So we just got home from Andrew's last night at Mob Middle School. Everyone threw him a going-away party in the cafeteria. Well, every mob EXCEPT Bones and his buddies. Bones has steered clear of Andrew since the Herobrine incident. (MISSION ACCOMPLISHED.)

I pretty much accomplished ALL of my missions in my 30-Day Plan. I mean, I did learn more about hockey. And Cate helped me give Andrew a killer makeover—to make him look like Herobrine. And I got inside that locked trunk and found a treasure, even if it wasn't the kind I was looking for.

But you know what? I never DID find out what Andrew was allergic to—at least, not until this morning.

See, I still had that newspaper article about Great-Great-Grandpa Gerald on my dresser. And when Andrew was packing up his things, the article fell off the dresser and landed upside-down on the floor. And the article on the BACK was all about ALLERGIES, and how mold on HOUSEHOLD PLANTS can lead to sniffling and sneezing.

And you know what one of the photos showed in that old article? A CACTUS.

Well, I pointed that cactus out to Andrew right away, and we both agreed that Mom could stand to ditch a few prickly plants around here.

Turns out, Andrew dislikes those dumb cactus plants as much as I do. REALLY? I guess we DO have a few things in common.

I mean, we both like sleepovers. And we're both kind of into Herobrine these days. And if Andrew were sticking around for another week or two, who knows? Maybe we'd find even MORE things we both like. Yup, we probably would.

Anyway, Mom got all teary-eyed when she saw Andrew packing. Then she let it slip that she's planning one more Saturday night dinner with special guests.

Andrew looked as freaked out about that as I felt, so I guess that's one more thing to add to the list. (We're both terrified of Mom's Saturday night dinners.) But then Mom said her "special guests" would be Andrew and his family, all the way from Humanville. YAAASSSSS!

So I guess I'll be seeing some more of the dude. Maybe by the time he comes back, Dad and I will have that hockey rink all cleaned up and ready for action. Or . . . maybe we won't. But either way, Andrew and I will figure out something fun to do.

Or maybe we'll just hang out.

You know, like brothers.

DON'T MISS ANY OF GERALD CREEPER JR.'S HILARIOUS ADVENTURES!

MOB SCHOOL SURVIVOR
THE CREEPER DIARIES
GREYSON MANN
ILLUSTRATED BY AMANDA BRACK

CREEPER'S GOT TALENT
THE CREEPER DIARIES
GREYSON MANN
ILLUSTRATED BY AMANDA BRACK

CREEPIN' THROUGH THE SNOW
THE CREEPER DIARIES
SPECIAL EDITION
GREYSON MANN
ILLUSTRATED BY AMANDA BRACK

NEW CREEP AT SCHOOL
THE CREEPER DIARIES
GREYSON MANN
ILLUSTRATED BY AMANDA BRACK

THE OVERWORLD GAMES
THE CREEPER DIARIES
GREYSON MANN
ILLUSTRATED BY AMANDA BRACK

CREEPER FAMILY VACATION
THE CREEPER DIARIES
GREYSON MANN
ILLUSTRATED BY AMANDA BRACK

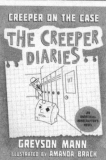

CREEPER ON THE CASE
THE CREEPER DIARIES
GREYSON MANN
ILLUSTRATED BY AMANDA BRACK

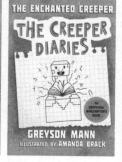

THE ENCHANTED CREEPER
THE CREEPER DIARIES
GREYSON MANN
ILLUSTRATED BY AMANDA BRACK

SKY PONY PRESS

Sky Pony Press
New York